The Leopard and the Galogalo

By Rotimi Ogunjobi

Auntie Mimie Children Series

© 2013 Rotimi Ogunjobi

ISBN: 978-978-49837-3-0

AUTHOR'S ACKNOWLEDGEMENT

The story in this book was adapted from several Yoruba folk tales.

Purchase Enquiries:

Xceedia (Media and Publishing) Ltd.

publishing@xceedia.co.uk

CONTENTS

Rotimi Ogunjobi

Galogalo Meets Leopard

Long ago, there was a very strange-looking and cunning creature which looked like a fox, but also had a shell on its back like a tortoise. The animal was called Galogalo. Even though it was neither strong nor fierce, all other animals avoided Galogalo because it was a very crafty creature. One of its favourite tricks was to make friends with a small animal and thereafter lead it to the lion's den. And when the lion came out, Galogalo would quickly climb up a tree, because it could climb very well, leaving the other animal behind to its sad fate.

Somehow Galogalo and Leopard became good friends, and all that the other animals could do was watch; some in amusement and some with anxiety. When Leopard's wife went out one day, she overheard some animals talking about the strange friendship between her husband and Galogalo, and she decided to find a way to end this friendship. When she got home, she called her husband and said to him:

'My dear husband, mighty one of the jungle, come closer to me for a heart-to-heart discussion. What is it with you and Galogalo? Why does he come here so often? There is really nothing that you both have in common as far as I can see, as you are not related in any way. What is it then that makes you to love this ugly creature so much that you are both seen together in all places as if you are engaged to be married? I am nearly always ashamed to go out anymore for the shame of the other animals saying spiteful things behind you. I want you to stop Galogalo from coming to this house.'

This was what Leopard's wife said to him. But animals will always be animals and instead of Leopard to listen to his wife and to be patient with her, he punched her on the cheeks. In response his wife bit his ears and he again bit her on the nose. A bitter fight was the result. And so were their many years of friendship destroyed because of Galogalo. Leopard's wife was pregnant at this time, and sadly as a result of this fight, when the child was born it was born a hunchback. When leopard's wife saw that her husband would not listen to her advice about Galogalo, she decided not to talk about it anymore.

One day Galogalo came to Leopard for a visit. Leopard has just killed a gazelle, which he shared with Galogalo, and not even a bit of it was given to Leopard's wife to eat. And after they had finished eating, Galogalo said to Leopard:

'My dear friend, Leopard, you are second only to the lion in this forest and a great leader amongst all the other animals. I am really so happy that I am your friend, but as you know, our marvellous relationship does not please so many people. Regardless of what they say however, our friendship will never come to an end, because it was made in heaven. Let us therefore be happy together every day for this and let the scorners die in their anger. I love you above all things and above all persons in this world, and if you were a woman I would gladly marry you. But even though you are not a woman and so cannot be my wife, there are very many other ways that we may make each other happy. I will want to do you a favour that will make us friends forever, because I think our children should also be friends even long after us. I would wish to decorate your children with beautiful spots. But these spots will be different from what you will find anywhere. And when I am done all the animals in the forest will be left with no more doubt that you are the

'I love you above all things and above all persons in this world, and if you were a woman I would gladly marry you'

greatest of them all, and even Lion will see quite clearly that he is called king for nothing and he is really no match for you. I want all your daughters to be so beautiful that every animal will desire to marry them and whether Lion wants or not, he will also come to ask you for one of them for his child to marry.

Fox will bring hundreds of chickens just to please you; even the gazelle, graceful horns and all, will come to you to be eaten; so will elephant with his precious tusk. It is my desire that after I have finished painting beautiful spots on your children, you will become famous beyond all imagination. Eventually I shall one day call all the animals together, and when I have gathered them in one place we shall all agree together to remove Lion as king, and then you will rule over us all. This is the great wish that my heart has for you dear friend, and I want you to think well. Does it please you to let me paint spots on your children and let good fortune result from it; or shall we neglect to do this and let all the good fortune pass by?'

So did this mischievous animal present his evil suggestion, which Leopard accepted without thinking and then Leopard replied:

'My dear friend, my true friend, my real friend, my friend without question, my sweet friend, my friend in the morning, my friend at noon, my friend at night, my friend on earth, my friend in heaven, my friend that my entire body seeks, my friend who is better than my father, my friend who is better than my mother, my friend who is better than all my relatives, my friend who is greater than my wife, I thank you very much for all you have said and I am so amazed at the size of your love for me, and how you bring nothing but good cheer into my life every day. I have heard your suggestion, and as you know what belongs to me also has become yours, even as what is yours is also mine. Why then do you ask my opinion about this? If you think that my children should be painted with beautiful spots, then so be it. Let us therefore prepare for it. Whatever you will want me to bring to you for this, let me know.'

'Thank you,' Galogalo said with a hearty laugh after Leopard has finished speaking. 'It will normally be important that we purchase a lot of items that are necessary for this task. But do not worry, I will buy them because you are my friend. Only build a small house not too far away from your house and near the river, and this house will have only one window and one door. In the house you will place a sharpened axe and a sharpened knife. And when you have finished I will take my ink to the little house that you have built near the river, and there I shall live with your seven children for seven days and there I shall paint beautiful spots on them.'

A very wide river separated the house of Leopard and that of Galogalo. It was near the bank of this river that Leopard built the small house as Galogalo had described - with one door and one window. And so, thereafter arrangements were made for the painting of spots on Leopard's cubs.

Galogalo Kills Leopard's Cubs

Before the day that the painting would commence, Galogalo had taken some cooking oil to the little house near the river, and when the day came, all of Leopard's cubs were brought to this evil animal at the little house near the river. This was all in spite of the desperate pleas of Leopard's wife which her husband had refused to give any regard to. As usual a fight had resulted, and Leopard had bitten off his wife's lower lip and the wife had in turn whacked him on the head with a heavy stick. It was indeed such a bitter fight that Leopard's children ran off to fetch elephant and gorilla to stop them.

On the day that the Leopard's cubs were taken into the little house by the river, Galogalo painted bright spots on the body of one of them. He did this so marvellously well and the child indeed looked very beautiful. On the second day however, he killed one of the Leopard's children for food, and so did he again on the third day and on the fourth, fifth, sixth and seventh day, until all that was left was one that he had painted. Galogalo was indeed very well fed for the seven days.

On the morning of the seventh day, as he opened the only window of the little house he saw Leopard and his wife standing eagerly outside. When he saw them, he greeted them heartily, but told them to stand further back, because according to the custom of painting spots on the skin if they came too close too soon the spots would go bad. Therefore Leopard and wife should stand back and he would show them the children one after the other from the window; and they did so.

After this Galogalo lifted the only cub left alive and showed it to them through the window, and when they saw it they were overjoyed because the cub indeed looked very beautiful.

'You evil woman, did I not tell you that he is a very good friend? Shame on you,' Leopard harshly said to his wife. Galogalo put the cub down out of sight and then again lifted it up as before.

'Look this is the second one,' he gleefully announced to the parents. And again, Leopard and wife rejoiced. This Galogalo did seven times to the great delight of Leopard and wife.

'You must wait for seven minutes after I have departed from here before you enter this house to take the children away or the spots will go bad,' Galogalo advised Leopard; and having said this, he came out of the house.

Leopard thanked Galogalo for his help and gave him a sheep as a gift in appreciation. Then he walked with Galogalo to the river, where Galogalo hired a boat to take him to his home on the other side of the river. At the bank of the river they found several boat drivers and according to the custom at that time all of them were fishes. As much as all the able-bodied fishes pleaded with Galogalo to be hired, to the surprise of Leopard, the evil creature selected the only driver that was almost completely deaf out of them all.

And when Galogalo had climbed into the boat, he turned to Leopard and said to him.

'Goodbye fellow, go see your children now. Whatever you see however, do not let your heart be too sad. I have eaten so much meat that my jaws now ache and I must go home to give my teeth some rest. My greetings to your wife.'

'I do not understand, please say that again.' Leopard was truly perplexed. But Galogalo ordered the deaf fish to move the boat on its way and the fish obeyed and paddled off. As the boat coasted away Galogalo said again to Leopard:

'I said you should go home. I have eaten so much meat that my jaws now ache and I must return to my own home so that my teeth may rest.'

'What meat? Please say that again I do not understand,' Leopard again asked, still confused. Finally, from far away in the middle of the river Galogalo shouted to Leopard:

'You fool, return to your home. I said I have eaten all your children, bones and all, and their juicy thighs were quite nice and tasty. '

On hearing this, Leopard dashed to the little house and there found only one very scared cub and a lot of bones on the floor. He roared for his wife and in mad rage they both raced to the bank of the river; and there they roared for the deaf fish to return immediately with Galogalo. But as the fish could not hear, it could do no more than ask Galogalo what the spectacle was all about.

'Leopard and his wife said you are not rowing quickly enough, and if you do not make haste to the other side of the river they would certainly kill you when you return,' Galogalo lied.

And seeing Leopard and his wife weeping bitterly as they rolled in the dust, the deaf fish again:

'Master, what is the matter with them?'

'Leopard and his wife are extremely angry that they are this very moment preparing to come after you; and today you will certainly end up in a soup pot if you do not take care.' Galogalo told the fish. So the deaf fish rowed with all its might, taking Galogalo away towards the other side of the river. But even as they came near the bank Galogalo said to the deaf fish:

'You foolish fish, I feel quite sorry for you, and I advise you to row with more vigour. Leopard will soon be here and I would not wish to find your head in his cooking pot tonight; because if he catches up with you, you shall certainly die. As I see, you have so many children to take care of. If Leopard lays his hand on you that will be the end for you, and in an instant all your children will be left without a father and your wife will become a widow; therefore for your own sake row as hard as you can.'

So said the Galogalo and so the deaf fish rowed as fast as it could. As the boat coasted smoothly over the river, Leopard wept bitterly on the other side and his wife rolled in the dust in utter distress. And as this went on Galogalo

'The deaf fish rowed as fast as it could. As the boat coasted smoothly over the river, Leopard wept bitterly on the other side.'

laughed merrily, and the deaf fish rowed with all its might. They soon reached the other side of the river and Galogalo paid the deaf fish. The fish thanked him and departed into the deep water of the river.

'My foolish friend on the other side of the river,' Galogalo called out to Leopard. 'Sorry for all your troubles. Why is your wife rolling in the dust? You must advise her to roll away from the river, for if she is not careful she will certainly end up in the water. I want to tell you a secret; your children were really delicious. I ate the oldest of them three days ago; his bones were a little too hard but I eventually cracked them; he was very tasty. It is the youngest one that I enjoyed most; his bones were soft and quite juicy. I will never forget the lovely taste of his head; brain, bones and all. Farewell; if on another day I again become very hungry, I shall come to your house and if do not yet have any new children I shall certainly not mind to eat from your relatives. Goodbye dear friend.' And so went Galogalo to his home.

After a while Leopard took his wife and led her home. The sad story spread quickly amongst all the animals, and even the smallest of them laughed at Leopard's folly; but the bigger animals were not so amused and their sympathy was with Leopard for the great loss and tragedy which had befallen him. The elephant came to visit him, so did the hyena; lion the king had sent a messenger; the domestic animals would have sent representatives, but when they discussed this in a meeting at the suggestion of the cat, the sheep disagreed and so did the cow. And when the dog who was chairman of the meeting suggested a vote, asking that all animals in agreement to send a representative should wag their tail, only a few did.

Leopard Plans to Revenge

As Leopard thought everyday about what Galogalo had done to him, he could not take his mind off the thought of a suitable revenge. Soon after, Leopard killed a gazelle and took it to the king as a bribe, pleading for the king's support to bring Galogalo to justice. They both finally decided that the king would send a town-crier to ring a bell all round the town and to announce that the king wished to decorate his palace. All animals would be asked to bring fresh leaves for decorating the king's palace; the punishment for an animal that did not do this would be to be sent away from the town. But the leaves were of a special kind, and could only be found in a particular part of the forest, and there the king has told Leopard to go wait.

Galogalo heard the king's message and as he was a very wily animal he knew that it was all a plan to trap him. So in the middle of the night he went with his wife to the place where the leaves grew. Together they picked a large bundle of the leaves and then Galogalo hid in the middle.

Ensuring that he was completely covered, he asked his wife to take a rope and make a parcel of him and the leaves. This Galogalo's wife did this and then she returned home leaving Galogalo and the leaves behind.

Galogalo knew for certain that Leopard in his eagerness to catch him would be the first to arrive at this place where the leaves grew. And even as he expected, no sooner had his wife left that he heard the voice of Leopard.

'The dunce has not come yet; but I will claim this parcel of leaves that another fool had carelessly left behind, and then I shall wait for him. When the person who owns this parcel eventually comes I am sure he would not even try to take it away from me. After all am I not the Leopard, prince of the jungle, and does anyone dare cross me even amongst all the animals?' Leopard said to himself.

So Leopard sat near the bundle of leaves, watching all the other animals come and go and in the hope that Galogalo would also be amongst them. But all the animal came and left and his waiting was all in vain. When he was again alone after all the animals had left, and Galogalo had still not come, he sighed and started to leave with the parcel of leaves on his back. After a while

Galogalo reached out from within the leaves and pulled Leopard's hair.

'These leaves do have so many thorns on them,' Leopard grumbled; not knowing what had happened. After a while Galogalo again spat on Leopard's head.

'There is really so much dew on these leaves,' Leopard again grumbled to himself. So did Galogalo continue to mischievously torment Leopard all along the way to the king palace. And when the king asked Leopard how well their plan had gone, Leopard could only reply with sadness and disappointment that Galogalo had failed to come.

After Leopard had left the palace, Galogalo came out of the parcel of leaves and tied it up once more. Then he went into the king's palace and said to him:

'Your majesty, I have brought my own gift of leaves, and it was indeed very heavy. Nevertheless, I bore it on my head out of love for you. After all are you not the father of all animals both of the jungle and of the towns and villages? You are indeed father to all of us, your majesty; do accept my humble gift.'

So did Galogalo say to the king and the king completely puzzled, could do nothing more than thank him. Galogalo was indeed a really nasty animal, and the next day he went to the river and called to Leopard in the other side.

'Good morning, my foolish friend. How heavy was the parcel of leaves that you took to the king yesterday. It has not broken your back, has it?'

'I thought you will be brave enough to come to the leaf farm yesterday. It would have been your last day on earth,' Leopard angrily roared back, but Galogalo laughed.

'I surely was there, my foolish friend, I was there only you did not see me. I did know that it was because of me that the king ordered all the animals to the farm. I was hiding in the leaves that you took to the king. Do you remember that you thought there were thorns in the leaves? It was me pulling your hair, and when I spat on your head, you thought the leaves were dewy, and when you finally reached the king's palace and went away to your own home, it was then that I came out of the leaves to greet the king.'

And when the Leopard heard this, he returned home very sad and unable to eat for the entire day. 'Do you know that I carried Galogalo to the king's palace yesterday?' Leopard told his wife when she insisted to know what the matter was.

'Who?' the wife was very surprised to hear.

'Galogalo,' Leopard sadly replied.

'How did that happen?' The wife wanted to know

'Can you believe that he was hiding in the leaves that I took from the farm to the king? When I got to the farm I found a parcel of leaves that someone seemed to have left behind and I took it. I did not know that Galogalo was hiding inside it.'

'You went to the farm; you found a parcel of leaves and took it, without any care for the owner or about what else could be in it? Well, if you take what doesn't belong to you, then you should be ready to receive problems that shouldn't belong to you,' his wife scolded him. And when Leopard heard this from his wife, he was again seized with anger.

'What do you think I should do?' He asked his wife.

'Go again to the king and find another way to punish this evil creature,' his wife told him.

Leopard took his wife's advice, and the next day he told the king all that had happened. The king listened, and he was quite amazed.

'This animal certainly intends to completely destroy you; but return home and let us discus it once more in two days,' the king said to Leopard.

Galogalo at the Big Feast

The next day, Leopard killed two gazelles and again sent them as another bribe to the king, and the king was pleased with him. And so on the appointed day, Leopard went to the king, and again they prepared a new plan to capture Galogalo. The plan was for the king to call all the animas to a feast. A special invitation was to be sent to Galogalo and he was to be invited as an important guest. This they thought should be a sure plan because Galogalo could never resist food, and secondly it would be such an act of dishonour for anyone to disregard the king's invitation. Leopard agreed to pay for the feast.

Thus the king sent special greetings to Galogalo through two ministers and two important Chiefs who were highly respected by all the animals. They were accompanied by two soldiers, two royal maidens, and two palace guards. He also ordered that an announcement should be made for all the animals to come to the palace for a feast in nine days.

'Tell Galogalo not to be surprised to see the king's messengers, and that this is because the king loves him so much, wants to make him a good friend, wants to give him a key to enter the palace as he wishes, and to be much honoured amongst all the animals,' the king sent in his message to Galogalo. When the messengers got to Galogalo's house, he did not give any impression that he knew what was afoot. He welcomed them heartily, and sent then away with message to the king that he would certainly be at the feast on the appointed day, and in his best clothes.

After they had left, Galogalo found twelve giant rats. He gave them money and a lot of food, and asked them to dig a tunnel, from his home to the king's bedroom in the palace. And without questions the rats started the work of digging the tunnel, working on it night and day. Galogalo also went to the birds and borrowed from them feathers of all sizes and colours.

Before dawn on the day of the big feast, Galogalo woke his wife. They took gum which he had collected from trees in the forest and covered his body with the sticky substance. He then instructed his wife to stick the feathers onto his entire body except for the face and legs. After this he painted his face and legs with chalk, and then put on boots of shiny brass. Thus disguised he looked nothing like Galogalo, and so did this animal prepare himself for the feast. And as all the other animals gathered together at the palace, Galogalo entered the tunnel and journeyed inside it to the king's room in the palace. Making sure that there was nobody in the bedroom, he left the tunnel and entered the room from beneath the king's bed. After a minute Galogalo raised a loud cry.

'Attention all! Attention all! I am the king's father and I have come from the other world! Attention everybody!'

And when the animals heard this they all fell silent and all eyes were turned towards the palace door. Having arrested their attention Galogalo pulled open the palace door and stepped out. And when the animals saw the strange creature, many fled in fear, but Galogalo told them not to be afraid.

'I am the father of the king, and was just unable to contain my happiness and that is why I have come today to rejoice with my dear son on the day of this feast.'

As he spoke as if through his nose, nobody knew that it was Galogalo because he spoke as if

'Attention all! Attention all! I am the king's father and I have come from the other world! Attention everybody!'

through his nose, like a real spirit from another world was believed to do. And to the rest of the animals he certainly sounded and looked like the dead father of a king because they had never seen such a strange creature. And so they danced and rejoiced around him; and even the king joined in the dancing. The crowd indeed felt so fortunate on this day to have the dead father of the king visit them, and any of them that Galogalo smiled at would take the memory to the grave. Elephant danced till the tress around began to fall, Leopard danced so heartily that two of the smaller animals were trampled to death. Monkey jumped and somersaulted so much that his head was badly bruised, the gazelles lost his horns dancing. There was so much joy around on this day and especially for the king because his dead father had come to visit from the other world.

After a while, Galogalo asked for food, and the king quickly ordered that he be given the best of all the food. When the food came, Galogalo called Leopard.

'Come feed me the food with a spoon,' Galogalo ordered, and Leopard felt so honoured above all the other animals. After a few minutes of this task, Galogalo ordered Leopard to stop.

'Go and cut those silly sharp nails, or don't you have any shame? Even if you have none do you not realise that your sharp nails could scratch my mouth?' he scolded and Leopard quickly did as he was ordered and cut his sharp nails.

After the fake father of the king had eaten and he was full, he said good things about Leopard to all that were gathered around.

'I certainly like the way he put the food into my mouth; it is just the way I like to be fed. Therefore before I go away I will reward him with mighty powers even before all of you gathered here.' Then he asked Leopard to hold out his hands. As Leopard did this Galogalo put a large lump of stinking mud on the hands, spat on it and mixed it all up with a little stick.

'In your hands you have a very precious substance - it is a present from the other world. Rub it on your head and marvellous things will begin to happen to you from this day. And this Leopard did joyfully, rubbing the stinking substance all over his head. His head indeed became quite horrible to look at; it also stank so much that hundreds of flies buzzed all about him and covered his entire body. Again Galogalo asked Leopard to hold out his hands. He spat on the hands and ordered Leopard to rub the spit all over his face. And this Leopard also did quite happily.

Leopard happily went along with all this humiliation believing that he had been selected to be specially honoured by the king's father. And this went on all through the feast and till nightfall after which Galogalo mischievously said his blessings on all that were assembled, and went back home through the tunnel that was under the king's bed in the palace, well fed and happy with himself.

The next day after Galogalo had taken off his disguise and washed himself clean, he again went to the river and called out to Leopard on the other side.

'Good morning, my foolish friend. How was the feast at the king's palace yesterday?'

'How dare you talk to me, you horrible creature? You knew of course that your evil deeds pursue you everywhere and they prevented you from seeing the wonders that we all witnessed yesterday. But go ask all the other animals anyway and they will tell you. I may not appear so important to you but all the other animals will tell you differently. I am honoured by those in this world and even those in the other world.

Everybody will tell you how the king's father from the other world selected me to be specially honoured yesterday. If only you were brave enough to come near me, you will see traces of the marvellous substance that he gave me to put all over my head, and even the king was not so honoured. I feel sorry for you, poor evil animal, pursued everywhere by your many evil deeds and missing out on all the good things of life. But no matter how much you run and hide, one day I shall certainly catch you, and that will be the end of your evil life.'

This was what Leopard said to Galogalo, but Galogalo only laughed and to Leopard's great sadness showed him a handful of the feathers he had worn the previous day.

'Leopard, you are indeed a very simple person and it is I that should pity you. You come after me for vengeance because you imagine that because I am smaller than you, I should be easy to capture. There was never any king's father; it was I dressed up as the king's father. Look at the feathers which I made into a coat. See the chalk with which I painted my face and body. I spread smelly muck on your head, and my spit on your face. Here are the brass shoes that I wore. And thank you for feeding me with food like a king, and removing your sharp nails when I ordered you to. See how much you have suffered for your foolishness. Go tell your dear wife again what I did to you after I ate all your children. I pray that you will one day be delivered from your many miseries and especially from my hands but that will not be by my death, because I am wiser than you.'

And Galogalo went away from the river leaping and dancing and singing a song about how he had made rub his spit on Leopard's head. Leopard also went back home weeping to his wife.

'Wife, did you know that I rubbed Galogalo's spit all over my head?' he rumbled with great anger.

'You did what?' his wife was puzzled.

'I rubbed Galogalo's spit all over my head yesterday at the feast,' he roared. They looked at each other silently for a while deeply saddened. But the sadness became too much for his wife to bear, that she shouted aloud for everyone to hear.

'Save me from this shame neighbours! Galogalo rubbed his spit all over my husband's head. This shame will certainly kill me!' she cried.

And because her grief was much, Leopard's wife urged her husband to go quickly to the king's house and tell him all that had happened. And away went Leopard sadly. And when he got to the palace, he told the king everything that he had heard from Galogalo. It all sounded so amusing a tale that the king burst into laughter. He looked at Leopard's head and there was still some of the dried mud left on it even though Leopard had attempted make himself clean; and this made the king to laugh even harder to Leopard's annoyance.

'I think there is still a bit of it at the back of your head,' the king told him.

'Yes, I have rubbed my head so hard many times on the trees, and my head is so sore,' Leopard replied.

After the king had stopped laughing he began to seriously consider how to see the end of Galogalo. To him the animal had become too much of an embarrassment and a danger even to him the king. First of all, it was an act of rudeness to the king for an animal to be invited to the king's feast and he did not show up, and for the king to go kneeling before him in the belief that he was the king's long dead father. Galogalo was indeed becoming a threat to the king's position as the king.

Death of Leopard and Galogalo

It was finally decided that the king should pretend that he had heard nothing. The king made a plan to call Galogalo and show him a sack inside which Leopard would be hiding; and the king would order Galogalo to go wash the contents at the river. And so a few days later the king called Galogalo and showed him the sack.

'Go wash the content and bring them back to me,' the king ordered. Galogalo agreed and took the huge sack away in a cart. But all the while Galogalo suspected that it was Leopard hiding inside the sack. After he has left the palace, he found a strong rope and tied up the mouth of the sack, so tightly that it was impossible for Leopard to escape.

Having done this he went whistling away with the sack. On a cart he soon got to a blacksmith's forge and there he stopped. He felt the sack all over and soon found where Leopard's head was. Then he went into the shop and begged the blacksmith for a hammer. Whistling, he took the heavy hammer outside and with all his strength brought it crashing down on Leopard's head, killing him instantly. Then he went to the river, washed the empty sack and returned it to the king.

The king accepted this sack with both shame and fear, and he could not ask what had happened to Leopard. So the king went away into his palace and Galogalo also went away whistling to his home. At home he made a fire and roasted Leopard on it. He cut up the flesh and his wife made stew. Looking at Leopard in his stew pot filled Galogalo with so much relief and satisfaction that a large part of his troubles were over and so he went for a stroll.

At the blacksmith's forge, he found Dog outside pumping the bellows because Dog was the blacksmith. It looked so much fun to Galogalo he asked Dog if he could also pump the bellows. And as he gleefully pumped he began to sing a song about the stew pot in his house filled with Leopard's meat.

After hearing the song, Dog told Galogalo that he was going to do some other chores in the garden at the back of the forge. But this was not true because Dog headed quickly for Galogalo's house instead.

'As he gleefully pumped he began to sing a song about the stew pot in his house filled with Leopard's meat.'

'Your husband told me to fetch the pot of Leopard stew,' Dog told Galogalo's wife. She was surprised, but again she reasoned that this had to be true because it was only her and Galogalo who knew about the pot of stew. So Dog took the pot of stew and headed for his home. After eating as much as he could, he put the rest in his own pots and returned Galogalo's empty pot to his wife. Then he went back to his foundry, and there found Galogalo still pumping the bellows while singing his song about the pot of Leopard meat stew waiting for him at home. Dog also quietly returned to his work, hammering heartily at a piece of hot metal. After a while he asked Galogalo to take a rest, then he took the bellows and as he pumped he began to sing a song about how he had eaten up all the stew without leaving even a bit.

Galogalo was initially confused about the song but after a while his suspicion was stirred. He quickly said goodbye to Dog and hurried away home.

'Where is my pot of Leopard meat stew?' He called out to his wife as soon as he got home. His wife was again surprised.

'Was it not you that told Dog to come fetch it? You did not even give a thought to whether I should also have a taste; you ate it all with Dog. Don't tell me that this is not true, because how else could Dog have known that you had a pot of Leopard stew unless you had told him?'

When Galogalo heard this, he roared in anger, so loudly that the entire house shook. Then he sat down and wept bitterly because of his loss. What could he do? Of course he could not tell the king about it, so he headed instead for the court.

And when he told the court what had happened, he was careful not to tell them that Dog had eaten his Leopard stew, but only that Dog had stolen his food. He knew of course that if he had told the truth he would have been instantly killed, because Leopard was indeed very important to all the other animals.

After Galogalo had finished talking, the court sent for Dog so that they might hear his own side of the story and why he had done such a wicked thing as to steal Galogalo's food. But Dog was indeed wise; he had covered his entire body with smelly oil and was lying by the fireplace at his house when they came for him. In his cheeks he had also hidden raw eggs, one on either side of his mouth. When the court messenger came Dog lied that he had been ill for three months and hasn't set eyes on Galogalo for so long but the messenger insisted that Dog came along with him to court. And so Dog rose and hobbled along with a walking stick.

When he got to the court, the judge and jury were quite surprised because Dog indeed looked so ill.

'For three months, I have been ill and vomiting every hour,' Dog said to them. And as he said this he broke one of the raw eggs in his mouth and spat it out, and it did look like vomit. And so Fox was extremely angry that Galogalo had deceived the court and he immediately sentenced Galogalo to death.

And so they took Galogalo outside and beat him to death with clubs and stones. And when he was dead, they cut him into small pieces and all the animals shared the meat. This is how Galogalo met his end, in the same cruel way that he had dealt with others.

Questions:

1. What did the Galogalo look like?
2. Why did Galogalo take Leopard's cubs to the little house near the river and what did he do to them?
3. Why would you say Galogalo was an evil animal?
4. Leopard was unwise by attempting to get revenge. In what other ways had Leopard been unwise?

Some Words and Their Meanings:

1. **Cubs** – the young ones of a lion, leopard and some other wild animals.
2. **Coasted** – sail smoothly.
3. **Sympathy** – pity.
4. **Bribe** – money given some to make them do something.
5. **Parcel** – a bundle, box or packet of something.
6. **Tunnel** – a road or passage dug inside the ground or through a mountain.
7. **Somersault** – Jump and turn over in the air.
8. **Muck** – smelly dirt.
9. **Misery** – sadness.

10. **Embarrassment** – shame.
11. **Forge** – a blacksmith's work place or bench.
12. **Blacksmith** – a person who makes useful things from metal.
13. **Bellows** – the equipment used by the blacksmith to blow air into his fire.
14. **Foundry** – a blacksmith workshop

Another Book by the Author

Ajala the Terrible Child

and other stories

Rotimi Ogunjobi